MARIANNE BORUCH:

"Everyone's here: two-bit admini. a10v01
sad national or state agency holding forth, secret as prayer. What
minds they've kept intact these years! These persona pieces
declaim, shrug off, invoke and mourn the small large things that
stop us too: life, death, Sharpie pens not all that sharp, love's
'buckets of bees' turned ash. 'I am time's shrapnel' sings one
lackluster compatriot rigged to a harness above the flag at the
National Museum of American History, just doing his job.

It's Martone doing his job: ear to wind and ground, picking up
the weird, the epic, the comic, the poignant: all the ghosts."

SUSAN NEVILLE:

"The narrators in these memoranda invoke their rights: to
remain silent when it's called for, to speak only of what they
wish to. In these brief and lovely fictions, Martone reveals
that the best response to the gods' great silence is the hint that
implies the depth of our emotions, our understanding of the
joke. *Do you understand the rights I have just read to you?*
With these rights in mind, do you wish to speak to me? Yes,
these characters say to the universe. They wish to speak. And
yes, we say, we want, more than anything, to listen to them."

MEMORANDA

Memoranda

MICHAEL MARTONE

DURHAM, NORTH CAROLINA

MEMORANDA

Copyright © 2015 by Michael Martone

Published in the United States of America

———————

Library of Congress Cataloging-in-Publication Data

Martone, Michael
Memoranda: stories / by Michael Martone
p.   cm.
ISBN-13: 978-1-4951-5762-2

———————

BOOK DESIGN BY Flying Hand Studio
AUTHOR PHOTO BY Theresa Pappas

PUBLISHED BY BULL CITY PRESS
1217 Odyssey Drive / Durham, NC 27713
www.BullCityPress.com

M E M O R A N D A

RE : Dedication

———

TO : Melanie Rae Thon & Margaret Himley
    & Safiya Henderson-Holmes (in memory of)

The EPA Diver Mapping the Turbid Outflow

Emanating from the Tully Valley Mudboils,

Enters the Eutrophic Waters of Lake Onondaga

In the murk, there, a reef looms, ten meters deep.

Smashed shards of china. I find a cup intact.

Inside slosh silvered dregs of mercury.

A Surveyor Attached to the Seabees Halts
Construction in Wisconsin's Land-Locked
Chequamegon-Nicolet National Forest to
Assess an Unexpected Environmental Impact

Burying ELF dipoles, the backhoe buckets
mushrooms. One organism, this fungus,
2,000 acres, like the antennae we're installing,
like so many submarines in the dark.

While Soaking His Blistered Feet, a Forest Service
Forester, Serving at the Talladega National Forest,
Recounts for His Wife Some of the Forensic
Evidence Collected That Day

> Looking for the body, we found hundreds of
> burned-out light bulbs in a clearing. Found four
> bodies, but not the body we were looking for.

The Pregnant Attorney from the Office of the Legislative
Council Pauses in Statuary Hall Where John Quincy
Adams, It Is Said, Eavesdropped on the Opposition

The parabolic dome echoed — echoes they tried to
damp with scarlet drapes. I've heard its heartbeat.
The bill in my briefcase — stillborn.

An Analyst from the National Climatic Data Center

in Asheville, North Carolina, Visits the Grave

of the Author O. Henry

It all doesn't add up. Knowing more, we know

less. Along the Blue Ridge, that blue cloudbank,

disguised as smoke, it turns out, is smoke.

Near Amarillo, a Technician from Interior at the
Cliffside Storage Facility Monitors the Congressionally
Mandated Drawdown of the Helium Reserve

I've tried this before. Inefficient. Lighter than air air.

Death descends, weighs its way. You can hear it,

right, gaining ground, this squeak I speak?

*The US Army Corps of Engineers Hydrologist Attached
to the Engineer Research and Development Center's
Information Technology Laboratory Watches the
New Godzilla Movie in 3D*

> The 1:100 scale Mississippi River Basin Model
> decays outside Vicksburg. The simulation
> was more real than the real river. I'll stomp
> on "Vicksburg," backwater town.

In the Ditch, Minnesota I-35, a Biologist of the Twin Cities
Ecological Field Office, Fish & Wildlife Service, Plants
Milkweed, Asclepias meadii, *a Threatened Species*

This toxic meal ticket for caterpillar, *Danaus plexippus*.
This poisoned highway we're planting to Mexico.
This desert crowned by barbed fire, depleted
Monarchs hoboing south.

The Distracted Stenographer at the FAA Attempts to
Transcribe the Recovered Contents of the Cockpit Voice
Recorder Salvaged from the Wreckage of UAL Flight 444

...black box isn't black but orange not orange

more blood red not a box so much but

not not missed...

An Engineering Technician of the NanoFab Operations
Group at the Center for Nanoscale Science and Technology
of the National Institute of Standards and Technology in
Gaithersburg, Maryland, Attempts DNA Origami

Adenine/Thymine & Guanine/Cytosine. One long
scaffold strand folded/folded/folded/folded/folded/
folded/folded. How many folds, in half, before
the half cannot be folded again?

An Exterminator Working for the General Services
Administration in a Johns Hopkins Extension Evening
Creative Writing Class Considers Freytag's Triangle
While Regarding a German Cockroach

I thought that then (that there were four stages
to metamorphosis); forgot it during lunch;
I slept on it; then it came back to me.

A Clerk, Working for the Architect's Office, Flying the Flags Flown Over the Capitol of the United States of America, Sends Them Off to Constituents

It luffs, sags, as I haul it in, fold, send to a middle
school in the middle of nowhere. There, the
invisible's visible, I suppose.

The Comptroller of the United States Bullion
Depository Watches a Netflix DVD of Goldfinger
Again, Paying Particular Attention to Continuity

Wrong. Wrong. No, that's not... Stacked bars
crush the ones on the tier below. But there, that's
right. How did they? How did they know?

Checking the Agency's Master Calendar, a State
Department Diplomatic Attaché Explains to His
Curious Fiancée the Purpose of the Bolt of
Gingham Cloth in the Corner

Oh, that. The Salamanca Seneca's yearly treaty
obligation. I keep track of all those promises
promised — wampum, trinket — the symbolic stuff.
Mine to remember, remember?

At the Waffle House, an Assessor from the
Disaster Declarations Unit of the Federal
Emergency Management Agency Breaks
Crackers into a Bowl of Bert's Chili

> Think of this place as an index. Even roofless,
> it remains open. How bad can an EF5 be if
> one is still served risk-managed grits?

A Camoufleur at the Natick Soldier Systems Center
Digests Reports Finding Failure of the UCP Digitalized
Pixelated Pattern in Afghanistan

Mychildrenlookrightthroughme,throughthescreen
doorwhereIstandstill,foregroundflattenedintoback
ground,twenty-fivewords hiddeninthisoneword.

On Administrative Leave, the Postal Inspector Waits

in Line at the Sunrise, Maine, Post Office to Ask

If She Has Any Mail Held General Delivery

Even here, the end of the earth, wanted posters
are posted. Have you tracked me down? What
word's been sent? What, what do you want?

Downloading Text of Regulations from a Floppy Disk,
Still Utilized by the Government Printing Office
Typesetting the Federal Register, *a Compositor*
Considers the Word "Cliché"

> We're stuck in our ways. Who remembers the
> cliché? Cliché became cliché. Overused words
> got glossed. That big lead slug's familiar steely
> report clacking home.

The Keeper at the Claiborne Dam Near Monroeville
Reads To Kill a Mockingbird *Between Operating the*
Lock to Aid the Annual Migration of Spawning Fish

Paddlefish, blue suckers, Alabama shad, striped
bass, blue catfish, mooneye. It's fucking spring!
I lift cubic tons of fish, reverse the runoff, this
hydraulic shove.

*The Quartermaster at the General Services
Administration Practices Redaction on the
Staples Invoice That Records the Purchase of
Black Sharpie Pens Used for Official Redactions*

Too fine a point! I should have ordered a ruler
as well to splint this bold steady hand into the
flat black stretch of forgetting.

A Railroad Engineer, Not an Engineer Who Drives the Train but One Who Builds the Engine, Tests the New Deadman, Transportation Technology Center, Pueblo, Colorado

> Sad fact. This button must be constantly depressed. Constant depression. Simple physics. One pushes down and the earth pushes back. Don't. Don't. Don't. Don't. Stop.

The Incinerator Operator at the National Animal Disease Center in Ames, Iowa, Writes a Dear John Letter to Her Lover, a Beekeeper, Following the Bloom

> Colony Collapse Disorder eludes research. I burn
> buckets of bees. Enclosed, insects' ashes. That
> mailed anthrax powder, remember, was the
> "Ames" strain. Here, weaponized tears.

A Recently Manicured Chemist Running Tests at the
National Institute for Occupational Safety and Health
Dips a Finger in a Freshly Opened Oil Paint Can

To get that loud color, that safety yellow?
Lead chromate. It's the only way. Its aftertaste
is sweet like sponge cake. It stains the teeth.

A Conservator in the National Museum of American History Rigged into a Suspended Harness Floats Inches Above The Star-Spangled Banner

A star is missing. Someone's souvenir, lost long ago. I am time's shrapnel, saving spaces left out, restoring the nothing to the nothing left over.

Tuesday:

Boston Light:

Brewster Island: 42° 19' 40.85" N, 70° 53' 24.26" W

The Last Manned Lighthouse in the United States

The keeper writes when the light, flashing
white every 10 seconds, shines. *0123hrs.*
Seas: calm. Pressure: Falling. Skies: Severely.
Clear. Stars: Disappearing. 1 X 1

R E : **Acknowledgments**

F R O M : Michael Martone

T O : *Sonora Review, Faultline, Wigleaf,*
Negative Capability, Elsewhere,
and the anthology *Hint Fictions.*

C C : Paul Maliszewski & Hadley Ross, Legislative Consul.
Cheryl Dumesnil, Steve Fellner, Steve Featherstone,
Tobin Anderson, Deb Unferth, Jenny Colville,
David Rossman, Vincent Standley, Linda Perla,
Heidi Staples, Del Lausa, Lisa Howard, Roger Hecht,
Marilyn Wenker, Diana Joseph, David Keith, Danit
Brown, Sean Dougherty, Jennifer Reeder, Bryan
Fryklund, Matt Dube, Jane Binns, Paul Germano,
Tony Cook, William Tester, Roberta Bernstein &
all of the Transcribing Angels at Syracuse.

Peggy Shinner, Cyndi Reeves, Lisa Hadley, Sarah
Buttenwieser, Achy Obejas, Fred Arroyo, Robin Black,
Judy French, Shannon Cain, Samantha Hunt, Gabe
Blackwell, Rachel Howard, Erin Stalcup, Judy French,
Justin Bigos, Catherine Brown, & all of Swannanoa's
Attuned Fiduciaries. Michael Rosen, Michael Wilkerson,
Ann Jones, Steve Pett, Clare Cardinal, Joe Geha, Rosanne
Potter, John Crowley, Howard Junker, Sandy Huss, Louise
Erdrich & all Sundry Field Agents. John & Shelly Barth,
Librarians of my Babel. Sam Martone & Nick Pappas,
Clerks of my Heart. Theresa Pappas, Exchequer Deluxe.

BCC : Ross White & the Office of Engraving,
Superintendent Sublime.

31

Michael Martone was born in Fort Wayne, Indiana. He has taught at several universities including Johns Hopkins, Iowa State, Harvard, Alabama, and Syracuse. He participated in the last major memo war fought with actual paper memoranda before the advent of electronic email. Staples were deployed. The paper generated in that war stacks several inches deep, thick enough to stop a bullet. Martone learned that the "cc:" is the most strategic field of the memo's template, and he is sad to realize that fewer and fewer readers know what the "cc:" stands for let alone have ever held a piece of the delicate and duplicating artifact in their ink stained and smudge smudged fingers. It, like everything else, is history.